# Summer at Oak Tree Cottage

## by Anne Giulieri

raintree
a Capstone company — publishers for children

*Engage Literacy* is published in the UK by Raintree.
Raintree is an imprint of Capstone Global Library Limited, a company incorporated in England and Wales having its registered office at 264 Banbury Road, Oxford, OX2 7DY – Registered company number: 6695582

www.raintree.co.uk

Text copyright © Anne Giulieri 2017
Illustration copyright © Capstone/Galia Bernstein

Editorial credits
Gina Kammer, editor; Cynthia Della-Rovere, designer; Tori Abraham, production specialist

10 9 8 7 6 5 4 3 2 1
Printed and bound in China.

Summer at Oak Tree Cottage

ISBN: 978 1 4747 3159 1

# Contents

# Chapter 1
# An old cottage

As the car drove down into the valley, along the curved driveway, Olivia gazed out of the window. Through the tree trunks, an old wooden cottage appeared.

"I can see a house ahead," said Olivia.

"Yes, that's Grandpa's cottage. We're nearly there!" said Dad, as he carefully rounded the last bend.

There, next to an enormous oak tree, stood the little cottage. It had a small wooden veranda and a pointed roof. The steps were crooked, and the front door was old and worn.

The car pulled up beside the old cottage and the family began to unpack.

"It must have been so much fun for you growing up here, Dad!" said Olivia.

"It was great," said Dad. "Grandpa and I used to go fishing. We used to build things together, too. He was really good at making things with wood. He even made me that playhouse in the oak tree!"

"You were so lucky!" said Olivia.

"Yes, he was," replied Mum, smiling.

"Did you know that Grandpa grew up here, too?" asked Dad.

"Really?" said Samuel. "I didn't know that! The cottage must be old if Grandpa grew up here, Dad."

"Yes, it's really old," Dad answered. "And no one has lived here since Grandpa died a long time ago. But, we'll have all summer to get this place looking as good as new!"

## Chapter 2
# The hidden room

"Why don't you go and explore while I chop some firewood," said Dad.

"Take this torch just in case the lights don't work," added Mum.

Olivia and Samuel began to explore the little cottage. There was a kitchen, a bathroom and two tiny bedrooms. In the living room was a large stone fireplace, and what looked like a table and chairs under blankets. It all looked very strange covered up.

Mum was beginning to close the curtains as night was coming fast.

"What's in here?" said Samuel, as he opened a door. To their surprise, behind the door was a narrow staircase.

"Come on, Olivia, this looks interesting," said Samuel, as he shone the torch up the dark staircase. "Let's see what's up here!"

As Olivia and Samuel climbed the narrow staircase, the sound of Dad chopping wood became distant.

Olivia and Samuel were both excited as they reached the top of the stairs. They found themselves in a tiny room. The room was covered in dust and cobwebs and had a little window. They drew the curtains and looked out of the window, waving to Dad who was down below.

As they started to explore the room, they found old tools and books covered in dust. All of a sudden, something caught Samuel's eye.

"I wonder what this is," he said. Samuel carefully pulled out a box. It was no ordinary box! It was large and wooden and had beautiful carvings all over it.

"Let's open it," they both said at once, giggling with excitement.

## Chapter 3
# The box

"Well, you two have been busy, haven't you!" called Dad as he reached for the light. "I see you've found the attic!"

Olivia and Samuel looked up at Dad. "Come and see what we've discovered!" shouted Olivia.

As Dad looked on with interest, Olivia and Samuel began to remove items from the old wooden box. They were all amazed at what they found. They quickly realised that it was no ordinary box. In fact, it was a very special box!

The box held a cream-coloured baby blanket and a little teddy bear. There was a bag of marbles, a wooden train and silver coins. There was also a handwritten letter, two old photos and a tiny box. The marbles were brightly coloured, and the teddy bear was soft and cuddly.

"These things look really old," said Olivia. "I wonder who put them in here?"

"WOW!" said Dad, reading the letter. "It's Grandpa's time capsule!"

"Look at this beautiful tiny box," gasped Olivia. "I wonder what's in it?"

"Well, whatever it is, it must be special!" said Dad as he opened the tiny box. Inside was a photo of a boy and a scruffy-looking dog.

"Ah," said Dad. "That must be Milly. Grandpa always used to talk about her."

"And that must be Grandpa," said Olivia, pointing to the young boy in the photo.

"Who are these people?" asked Samuel, as he looked at one of the other photos.

"Let me see," said Dad. "Ah! This is a photo of Grandpa when he was young."

"Grandpa's family had an old car!" said Samuel.

"Well, it might look old to you!" explained Dad. "But back when Grandpa was younger, it would have been a brand new car."

"Things must have been very different when Grandpa was a young boy," said Samuel.

"Yes, they would have been very different," replied Dad. "He wouldn't have had the same types of toys that you have."

To whoever finds this letter.

I am 10 years old.

I have made a time capsule.

I have put some special things inside.

I hope you like it.

From Charles

# Chapter 4
# Samuel's great idea

"I have a great idea!" said Samuel excitedly, looking at Grandpa's photos. "Why don't we make our very own time capsule? We have all summer to do it!"

"That's a wonderful idea," replied Olivia. "We can put special things in our time capsule, just like Grandpa did!"

"Grandpa put in photos and things that he liked to play with!" said Samuel. "Maybe we can, too!"

The next morning Olivia and Samuel began making their very own time capsule. They looked at their toys.

"I'm not sure that I want to put my panda in the time capsule," Olivia said quietly. "I still like to sleep with him!"

"That's okay," said Dad. "But I'm sure you can think of some way to show that you had a special panda, without having to put him in the box. Just remember, a time capsule tells people in the future a story about you!"

As the days went on, they drew pictures, took photos and wrote some stories to put in the time capsule. The family also worked very hard fixing up the old cottage. Mum patched a hole in the roof while Dad worked on fixing the playhouse. Olivia and Samuel helped with painting.

One day the summer came to an end.
Their time capsule was finally ready.

"Where do you think we should hide our
time capsule?" asked Olivia.

"Well, we need a place where it can be kept
safe and dry," replied Samuel.

And with that, they both turned towards the playhouse in the oak tree and smiled. Once the time capsule had been hidden, they spent the afternoon relaxing. Mum, Dad and the children had worked very hard, and the old cottage had been brought back to life.

Oak Tree Cottage

"We've had so much fun at Oak Tree Cottage," said Olivia.

"Can we spend every summer here, Dad?" asked Samuel.

Dad smiled, "Of course we can. Grandpa would have been very happy to know how much we all love Oak Tree Cottage!"

Oak Tree Cottage